Two Shoes, Blue Shoes, New Shoes!

Two Shoes, Blue Shoes, New Shoes!

by Sally Fitz-Gibbon

Illustrations by Farida Zaman

Fitzhenry & Whiteside

Published in Canada by Fitzhenry & Whiteside,
195 Allstate Parkway, Markham, Ontario L3R 4T8

Published in the United States, 2003 by Fitzhenry & Whiteside,
121 Harvard Avenue, Suite 2, Allston, Massachusetts 02134

www.fitzhenry.ca   godwit@fitzhenry.ca.

10 9 8 7 6 5 4 3 2 1

National Library of Canada Cataloguing in Publication Data

Fitz-Gibbon, Sally, 1949-
Two shoes, blue shoes, new shoes / by Sally Fitz-Gibbon ; illustrated by Farida Zaman.

ISBN 1-55041-729-0 (bound).— ISBN 1-55041-731-2 (pbk.)

I. Zaman, Farida II. Title.

PS8561.I87T86 2002   jC813'.54   C2002-901607-X
PZ7

U.S. Publisher Cataloging-in-Publication Data
(Library of Congress Standards)

Fitz-Gibbon, Sally.
Two shoes, blue shoes, new shoes / by Sally Fitz-Gibbon ; illustrated by Farida Zaman.—1st ed.
[32] p. : col. ill. ;   cm.
Summary: A brand new pair of shoes can hop and skip to school better than anything.
And nobody is as proud of her shiny footwear as this little girl, who bounces and dances her way
through an imaginative adventure that only her two, new, blue shoes can discover.
ISBN 1-55041-729-0
ISBN 1-55041-731-2 (pbk.)
1. Shoes – Fiction. I. Zaman, Farida. II. Title.
[E] 21   2002   AC CIP

Fitzhenry & Whiteside acknowledges with thanks the Canada Council for the Arts, the Government of Canada through the
Book Publishing Industry Development Program (BPIDP), and the Ontario Arts Council for their support for our publishing program.

Book Design by Wycliffe Smith Design Inc
Printed in Hong Kong

To James, Michael, John and Allison and the memory of
Peter, whose feet all grew wings in their new shoes. And to
Janet, who allowed her children to soar.

– Sally

To mommy and daddy, who bought me my first pair of new shoes.
And for all little girls (and big girls, too) who love shoes!

– Farida

Two shoes,
blue shoes,
new shoes,

See what I can do, shoes!

Skipping down the street, shoes,

Look at who we meet, shoes!

**Mustn't stop to talk,
shoes,**

10

Got too far to walk,
shoes!

Swinging from a rope, shoes,

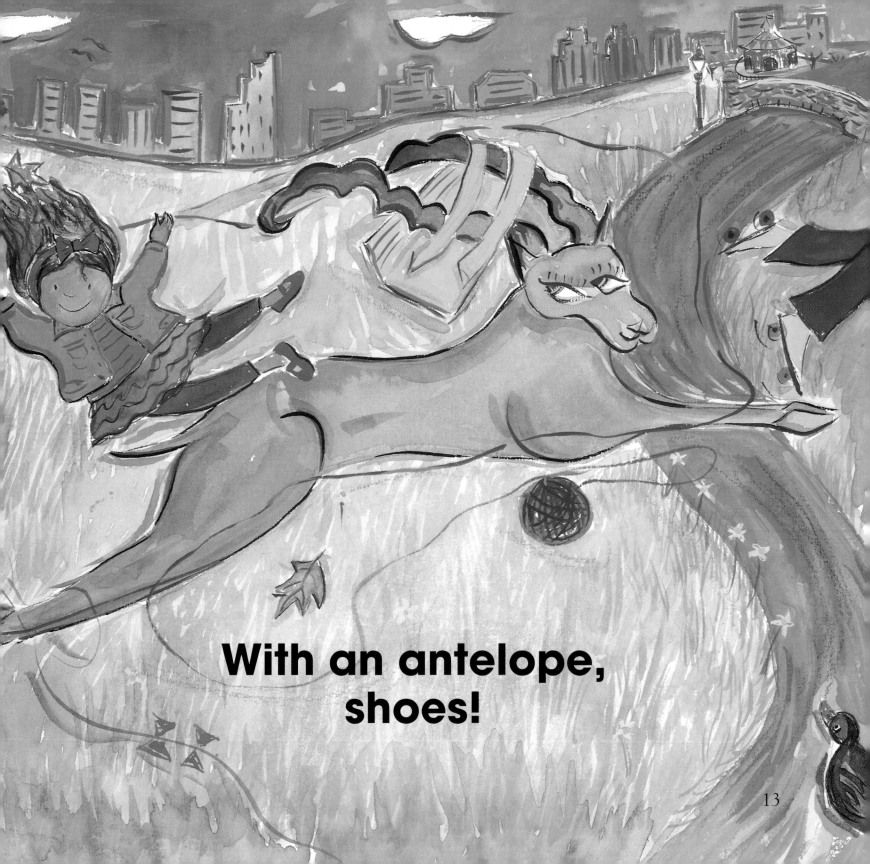

With an antelope,
shoes!

Riding on a whale, shoes,

14

See him splash his tail,
shoes!

15

Eating bread and cheese, shoes,

With two chimpanzees, shoes!

17

Jumping off a log, shoes,

18

Find a purple frog,
shoes!

19

Racing at the zoo, shoes,

Passed a kangaroo,
shoes!

Dancing on the moon, shoes,

With a blue baboon, shoes!

Bouncing on a cloud, shoes,

24

Whoops!
I'm not allowed,
shoes!

25

Tapping out a tune, shoes,

Will we be there soon,
shoes?

Peeking round the door, shoes,

28

Is there time for more, shoes?

29

Two shoes, blue shoes,
new shoes,

Going off to school, shoes!

Two Shoes, Blue Shoes, New Shoes!

Two shoes, blue shoes, new shoes,
See what I can do, shoes!

Skipping down the street, shoes,
Look at who we meet, shoes!

Mustn't stop to talk, shoes,
Got too far to walk, shoes!

Swinging from a rope, shoes,
With an antelope, shoes!

Riding on a whale, shoes,
See him splash his tail, shoes!

Eating bread and cheese, shoes,
With two chimpanzees, shoes!

Jumping off a log, shoes,
Find a purple frog, shoes!

Racing at the zoo, shoes,
Passed a kangaroo, shoes!

Dancing on the moon, shoes,
With a blue baboon, shoes!

Bouncing on a cloud, shoes,
Whoops! I'm not allowed, shoes!

Tapping out a tune, shoes,
Will we be there soon, shoes?

Peeking round the door, shoes,
Is there time for more, shoes?

Two shoes, blue shoes, new shoes,
Going off to school, shoes!

– Sally Fitz-Gibbon